The Lost Boys

Hook's Crew

Published by Hachette Partworks Ltd
ISBN: 978-1-906965-63-1
Date of Printing: June 2011
Printed in Singapore by Tien Wah Press

PETER PAN
RETURN TO
NEVER·LAND

DISNEP

Hachette

Once upon a time, a girl named Wendy met a magical boy called Peter Pan. He took her to a wondrous place called Never Land where nobody ever grows up.

When Wendy returned home, she promised, "I'll always believe in you, Peter Pan."

Years passed. Wendy grew up, but she never forgot her promise. Every night, Wendy told her two children stories about Peter Pan, the Lost Boys and a tiny fairy named Tinker Bell.

Wendy's daughter, a serious twelve-year-old called Jane, had no time for make-believe. But her brother, Danny, loved hearing the stories again and again, especially the one about Captain Hook and the stolen treasure.

Captain Hook and his men stole treasure from other ships. They kept their loot on their own ship, the *Jolly Roger*.

One night, Peter Pan and the Lost Boys slipped aboard the *Jolly Roger* and stole Hook's treasure.

It was all just a great game for Peter.

Peter and Hook had a long, fierce sword fight. Eventually, Peter and the boys escaped with the treasure. Then Tinker Bell showered the pirate ship with pixie dust, which made the *Jolly Roger* float off into the sky.

"You've not seen the end of me, Peter Pan. I'll get you for this if it's the last thing I do!" shouted Captain Hook as he drifted away.

"Hook will never win, as long as there is faith,
trust and pixie dust," Wendy said as she ended the
bedtime story.

Danny was delighted with the
tale, but not Jane. She thought
it was all just childish nonsense.
"Peter Pan isn't real, and people
can't fly," she declared.
"They do!" cried Danny.
"Oh Daniel, grow up!"
Jane said, and went to
her room.

Jane lay down on a seat next to the window. After a while, she fell asleep.

While she slept, something odd was happening in the sky outside. A strange visitor appeared, and it was someone she had never, ever expected to see...

Jane awoke to see Captain Hook standing there!

"Hello, Wendy," Hook said with a wicked grin. He thought he was talking to Jane's mother!

Before Jane could explain, Hook ordered his first mate, Mr Smee, to put her in a big sack.

"My apologies, Miss," said Smee, tying the sack.

Hook and Smee took Jane aboard the *Jolly Roger* and headed back to Never Land. Hook had a plan to trap Peter Pan once and for all.

"With Wendy as bait, we'll lure Peter Pan to his doom!" Hook bragged to Smee.

Luckily, just as the pirate ship arrived in Never Land, Peter Pan and Tinker Bell appeared.

Hook's men fired a cannonball at Peter. Of course, they missed.

So Hook pointed to the hanging sack. He boasted that he had captured Wendy and that he was going to feed her to the Octopus, who lurked in the water below.

"Let her go, you black-hearted scoundrel!"
demanded Peter. He and Hook began a
sword fight.

"You want her? Ha! Well, go and get her!"
shouted Hook.

Captain Hook raised his
sword and cut the rope that was
holding up the sack. To Peter's
horror, the sack plopped into
the water!

Bravely, Peter dived in to
save his friend. Tinker Bell
followed close behind, in case
Peter needed her help.

Captain Hook and the pirates peered eagerly over the side of the ship. After a moment, Peter's hat bobbed up on the surface.

Minutes later, when Peter still hadn't appeared, Captain Hook shouted triumphantly, "I did it! I'm free – free of Peter Pan forever!"

But Hook's delight didn't last very long.
Out of the water rose Peter Pan and Tinker
Bell! Peter flew off with the sack in his arms.

Tinker Bell sprinkled pixie dust onto the
giant Octopus, making it rise high above the
Jolly Roger.

Then Tinker Bell suddenly stopped sprinkling pixie dust. The Octopus landed right on top of Captain Hook with a loud *CRASH!*

Hook howled as the beast started to drag him over the side of the ship, back into the water.

The hungry Octopus was very pleased to have caught himself a Captain Hook dinner! But the captain was determined not to be the creature's next meal.

"Smee!" yelled Hook.

Smee grabbed Captain Hook's hand. Then Smee and the Octopus began a tug-of-war over Captain Hook!

Finally, with a mighty yank, Smee wrenched the captain out of the Octopus's tentacles. The two pirates flew through the air and landed in the cargo hold.

Smee had saved Hook. But the captain wasn't in the least bit grateful.

"Mr Smee, be a good fellow and fix the plank, please," Hook growled. "So that I can make you walk it!"

Meanwhile, Peter and Tinker Bell flew to safety.

Peter gently placed the sack on the ground and began to untie it. He couldn't wait to see his old friend, Wendy!

But when Peter opened the sack... *POW!*

Thinking she was still being held captive by the pirates, Jane had let loose a mighty punch.

"Ow! You're definitely not Wendy!" said Peter, rubbing his jaw.

Just then, Hook fired a cannonball at them. Peter flew off, with Jane in his arms.

"If you're not Wendy, who are you?" asked Peter.

"I'm her daughter, Jane," replied the girl.

As they flew over
Never Land, Jane was
amazed at all the sights
below her. Suddenly,
Peter stopped flying
and dropped Jane into a
hollow tree trunk.

Jane landed at the bottom
of the underground tree house
where Peter lived with the
Lost Boys.

Nibs, Slightly, the Twins, Cubby
and Tootles dropped down from the
ceiling to greet her.

"This is Jane!" Peter told the boys. "She's going to stay here and be our new mother and tell us stories!"

The Lost Boys gathered round Jane excitedly.

But Tinker Bell wasn't happy at all. She wanted Jane to go home. Tinker Bell didn't want to share Peter Pan's attention.

"Let's play a game,"
said Nibs.

"How about Treasure
Hunt?" suggested Peter.

But Jane didn't want
to play.

"No, no, no, no, NO!"
she shouted.

"I have to go home," Jane told them and
stomped off.

"What's the matter with her?" asked Cubby.

Peter scratched his chin and thought hard.

"I don't know," he said. "She acts kind of like
a grown-up."

"Ewwwww!" said the Lost Boys.

Peter followed Jane and soon found her building a raft so that she could sail home.

He watched as Jane pushed her raft into the water and jumped on board.

But she didn't get far!

Almost immediately, the raft began to break
up and sink. Jane fell into the water with a big
SPLASH!

When he saw that she was in trouble, Peter flew
out to save Jane.

"The only way out of here is to fly," explained
Peter. He set Jane down on the ledge of a huge rock.
"Anybody can do it," Peter assured her. All it took
was faith, trust and pixie dust.

But Jane refused to believe that she could fly.
Then Tinker Bell sprinkled some fairy dust on the
Lost Boys. They glided in the air around Jane, to
show her how it worked.

Peter asked Tinker Bell to
sprinkle Jane with pixie dust,
too, but Tinker Bell didn't
want to do anything to help
Jane! As far as Tinker Bell
was concerned, Peter liked
Jane too much!

Peter knew just how to persuade Tinker Bell.

"Gosh, if Jane can't fly, I suppose she'll just have to move in with us," he whispered to the tiny fairy.

Tinker Bell didn't like the sound of that at all! So she sprinkled Jane with lots of pixie dust. But all that happened was the pixie dust made Jane sneeze.

Now Peter was *sure* that Jane could fly. He nudged her off the ledge she was standing on, but Jane didn't have the faith and trust she needed to be able to fly.

"AAGH!" cried Jane as she fell. The Lost Boys tried to catch her, but they missed. Jane landed in the soft ground with a thud.

Jane was very angry.

"Leave me alone!" she yelled. "I don't believe in any of this, and I especially don't believe in fairies!"

As Jane stormed off, Tinker Bell began to flutter to the ground. She could no longer fly, and her light was fading fast.

Peter knelt down beside Tinker Bell so he could hear what she was telling him.

A worried Peter turned to the Lost Boys. "If we don't get Jane to believe in fairies," he told them, "Tink's light is going to go out altogether."

The group hurried off to find Jane.

Meanwhile, Jane came across Captain
Hook, who was weeping miserably. Hook told
Jane that Peter Pan had stolen his treasure.
Hook claimed that he needed the trcasure to
be able to afford to sail home to his mother!

The captain promised to take Jane home if
she helped him find the treasure, and Jane
agreed. Hook gave her a whistle, so
that she could alert him when she found
the treasure.

Jane didn't realise that she
had been tricked. Captain
Hook's real plan was to
capture Peter Pan!

Soon, Jane met up with Peter and the others. "Jane, I'm sorry," said Peter. "We want to do something to make it up to you. We want you to feel like you're one of us."

"Well," said Jane, "why don't we play Treasure Hunt?"

"Great idea!" said Peter. "But you'll have to think like a Lost Boy and have *fun* like a Lost Boy."

Jane couldn't
remember the last
time she'd had so much fun!
Eventually, she found the treasure.

Then Jane remembered Hook's whistle. She
realised that she didn't want to betray her new
friends, so she threw the whistle away.

Unfortunately, Tootles
spotted the shiny
whistle, picked it
up, and blew it
loudly!

"No, wait!"
cried Jane,
but it was
too late.

Captain Hook and the pirates heard the
whistle. In no time, they had captured Peter
and the Lost Boys.

Hook thanked Jane. "I couldn't have done it
without you," he told her.

"You're a traitor, Jane!" Peter shouted
angrily. "And because you don't believe in
fairies, Tink's light is going out!"

Hook took Peter and the Lost Boys back
to his ship. This time, he wasn't going to let
Peter get away!

Jane needed Tinker Bell's help, but she found the tiny fairy very weak. Jane started to cry.

"I'm so sorry," she said, because now she realised that she *did* believe in fairies.

Then something magical started to happen. Tinker Bell's light started to flicker. Soon, the fairy's light was shining brighter than ever before!

Jane and Tinker Bell got to the *Jolly Roger* just in time. Tinker Bell sprinkled Jane with pixie dust. Now that Jane believed she could fly, she *could* fly! She swooped away as Hook tried to grab her.

Jane managed to free Peter, but Hook hadn't given up trying to catch her.

"Gotcha!" bellowed Hook as he swung towards Jane on a rope.

But quick-thinking Peter grabbed his dagger and cut the rope. Hook plunged towards the water...

... and landed right on top of the Octopus!

"Smeeeeee!" wailed Hook as he tried to escape the beast's clutches.

"Let's hear it for Jane, the one and only Lost Girl!" the boys cheered.

Peter looked sad. "You can fly now. You can go home," he told Jane.

"I'll miss you," Jane admitted. "But now I have wonderful stories to tell, all about Peter Pan and the Lost Boys!"

Peter, Tinker Bell and Jane flew back to London.

At home, Jane and her family
were so happy to be back together.
Jane told her mother and Danny all about
her adventures in Never Land – the pirates, the
treasure, the giant Octopus, Tinker Bell and
especially Peter Pan.

Peter saw that his old friend Wendy was now a grown-up.

"You've changed," he told her.

"Not really. Not ever," Wendy smiled.

Wendy would always believe in Peter Pan. And now, after all her adventures, so would Jane!